THE CAMPOUT WASHOUT

Amanda,
You're going
to be the
best MOM
in the
world
—Love
Kyla

Mickey Mouse was going camping. He was really excited about it.

"I've been looking forward to this!" Mickey told Minnie as they packed the car.

"Me too," Minnie smiled, "wait until you taste the picnic Daisy and I made…"

"I've read all about campfires," Goofy told them.

"The tents are ready to go!" said Donald.

"I'm ready to go, too!" Mickey exclaimed. "Everybody hop in!"

Soon they were headed for a campground in the mountains.

"Doesn't the air smell great up here?" said Goofy. "Fresh and clean!"

Before long they arrived at a beautiful lake. "Let's set up right here!" said Mickey. "Where are the tents?"

Minnie and Daisy shook out the tents. Mickey searched for the poles. "I don't know where they could be…" he complained. "We must have forgotten to pack them!"

"Oh dear!" said Daisy. "What will we do? I'm starting to feel chilly already!"

"I'll build a big fire to keep us warm all night, and we can sleep under the stars!" offered Goofy.

"Great idea!" replied Mickey. "Let's all collect some firewood!"

They had a good time collecting firewood in the forest. It was hard work but kind of like a treasure hunt! Pluto was very good at sniffing out dry sticks.

Once Goofy announced that they had collected enough wood, they all stood back to watch him build the fire. "First, you need a circle made of rocks. Then, you pile the wood very carefully, like so…" he paused, "Now, we just need to light it…" Goofy rummaged in his pockets. "Did anyone bring matches?"

"It's okay, Goofy," Minnie told him. "We have nice warm sleeping bags. We'll be fine without a fire."

"Well, at least we still have our picnic," said Goofy. "I'm getting kind of hungry!"

They went to get the picnic basket, but the food had all been eaten! "A wild animal must have gotten into it!" said Mickey.

"Our roasted corn!" cried Minnie.

"Our tasty apples!" said Daisy.

"The chocolate cake!" moaned Goofy.

It was starting to get dark. "This is terrible!" Donald exclaimed. "No food, no fire, and no tent! At least I brought flashlights, so we can see…"

Donald took out a flashlight. He pushed the button, but nothing happened. He pushed it again. "Oh no," he said, "it needs new batteries!"

BOOM! Thunder filled the air and lightning flashed.
Rain started falling. "We can't sleep in a storm without tents!"
said Minnie.

"With no supper!" added Daisy.

"Or fire!" said Goofy.

"Or a flashlight!" Donald groaned.

Mickey stared at his wet friends and the stormy sky. "We can't stay," he said. "Let's pack up!"

They grabbed their things and ran for the car.

The storm grew worse as they headed home. The wind blew and rain pelted the car. Mickey was disappointed. He had been looking forward to camping, and so had his friends. But maybe there was something he could do about it…

By the time they got back to Mickey's house, he had it all figured out. "We're still going camping!" he told everyone, "but we're going to do it right here, in my living room!"

Everyone thought that was a wonderful idea!

Goofy got the fireplace going while Mickey found the poles and put up the tents.

Donald found some batteries for the flashlights.

Daisy and Minnie made another picnic and brought it into the living room.

The thunderstorm raged all night, but everyone stayed cozy and dry in Mickey's living room. They had fun making shadow figures on the wall with the flashlights and telling each other scary stories.

"That was a great picnic!" said Donald.

"This is a perfect fire for roasting marshmallows!" said Goofy.

"This is my favorite camping trip of all time!" said Minnie.

"Mine, too." said Mickey. "Home sweet home!"